First Summer
with Horses

First Summer with Horses

By: Heather L. Nelson
Illustrations by: Candace L. Diehl

authorHOUSE®

AuthorHouse™ LLC
1663 Liberty Drive
Bloomington, IN 47403
www.authorhouse.com
Phone: 1-800-839-8640

Published by AuthorHouse   10/25/2013

ISBN: 978-1-4817-7682-0 (sc)
ISBN: 978-1-4817-7681-3 (e)

Library of Congress Control Number: 2013912796

For All Horse-Loving People
And
Especially for Candace

AUTHOR'S ACKNOWLEDGEMENTS

I am grateful for the assistance of many people who contributed to the writing of this book.

I want to especially thank Candace Diehl (Kandee) whose memories, friendship, and editing suggestions help enhance the telling of these adventures. Her descriptive illustrations put the "eyelashes" on the book, as Dad used to say.

Thanks very much to my husband, Brian Nelson, for always helping in every way—then, and ever since.

A special thank you to Spence Diehl for his computer expertise and technical support.

Another special thank you to Donna Sanders for final proofing assistance and the first written review!

Thanks also to everyone who took the time to read the various drafts of this story and provide suggestions and helpful input. You all have wittingly or unwittingly contributed your expertise and assisted in the development of this book. I could not have written this without you.

ILLUSTRATOR'S ACKNOWLEDGEMENTS

I would like to thank my friend, Heather Louann, for writing this book about the most wonderful summer of my youth, and for believing in my "artistic abilities."

I thank my husband, Spencer, for taking over the chores and projects, which gave me the time to indulge in art and rediscover my artistic skills.

PROLOGUE

THE FIRST MEETING

"Wow, do you like horses too?" the two girls asked in unison as their school bus drove past a field of horses. They had just met and had their noses pressed against the window pane as the bus passed the horses.

"Yes, I love horses!" They replied in unison again as they turned to stare incredulously at each other. There was an instant feeling of kinship as if they had known each other for years.

The girls introduced themselves. "My name is Lou."

"I'm Kandee."

The day before, Kandee had noticed the new girl step on the bus, and then get off the bus before it arrived at school. Today, she decided to save a seat for her and find out what Lou was doing.

Both girls were in the eighth grade. Lou had just moved here from out of state. The local school was full, so she had to transfer to a school out of the region. Lou was allowed to ride the local school bus from her house to a point where she could transfer to another bus which took her to a different school. Kandee was curious about her.

The girls sat back on the bus seat and surveyed each other.

They each had a slight build. Lou noticed Kandee's very long, thin, light-brown ponytail and large, sparkling, dark brown eyes. Kandee had a very pretty smile that showed somewhat crooked teeth.

Kandee noticed Lou's crinkling blue-gray eyes, bouncy shoulder-length dishwater blonde hair and a sprinkling of freckles across her nose. They discovered that they both loved horses and spent their free time visiting every horse they could find within bike riding distance of their homes.

"Where I lived before, there were no horses close by. I rode my bike for six miles to visit a retired race horse. I tried to ride that horse and got bucked off twice. I haven't ridden a horse since," Lou stated dejectedly.

Kandee did babysitting and said she spent every cent she earned at riding stables. "I know the names of most of the horses and can show you which ones are the most fun to ride. I'll introduce them to you when I take you there sometime," she told Lou. "Also, we can come back and visit those horses we just saw in the field. Let's bring some carrots or apples. Treats are a great way to get them to come close." They continued to make plans and were so engrossed in talking about horses the rest of the ride that Lou almost forgot to get off the bus.

Kandee and Lou looked forward to their morning talks on the school bus which made the bus ride enjoyable and seemed to start the day off right.

After that first meeting, Kandee always saved a seat for Lou. Lou informed Kandee that her family was planning to buy a farm when school ended for the year, and she was going to get a horse. Kandee was excited and planned to ride it, too.

"I've been praying for a horse my whole life," Lou informed Kandee.

Kandee confessed she also prayed for a horse and every wish on a birthday cake was for a horse of her own. "But I don't see how it would ever happen. My family isn't planning to buy a farm. I'll have to get a job so I can have one. I don't mind because it's what I really want. Right now I mostly just read and dream about them, and visit any horse I can," she confessed.

A few weeks later, Lou's mom and dad announced they had found a small farm in the country. Their few acres were nestled amidst large farms with acres of berry fields. The house was small, but Lou's dad said he planned to build onto the house, build a better barn, and fence in the property. He was going to be busy. His dream was to raise cattle, so he bought a pregnant cow and kept it in the large back yard of their rental on the outskirts of the city.

Just before school was out, Betsy the cow had a calf. The girls named the calf "Barney". They thought he was so beautiful, with his white face and feet, and red coat. He had beautiful long, white eyelashes. Barney would suckle on their fingers as if he were searching for milk. The tickling sensation sent the girls into peals of laughter. At first, Betsy would eye them warily whenever the girls were near her baby, but she soon accepted the treats and the good rubs they gave her.

"School will be out in a few weeks so we better get busy and fix up the property. We will move to the farm then," Lou's dad stated a few days later. "Every weekend we need to go out to the farm to pull ferns and tansy since those plants are harmful for cattle and seem to be growing everywhere. We need to make the pasture safe."

"Those plants are not good for horses either," Lou interjected.

"Can I help?" asked Kandee, hoping they would say yes. "I know about tansy being a bad weed, and would be happy to help you get rid of it. Besides, it is always more fun to help with the farm chores than stay at home. My mother always told me many hands make less work."

Lou's mom and dad were amazed that Kandee wanted to help with the farm work. "Kandee is sure a nice girl," Lou's parents remarked. "I am so glad Lou found a good friend."

After that, Kandee joined Lou and her family every weekend to help on the property. Kandee loved going to the country and did not consider farm chores to be real work.

As they pulled the tansy and ferns, the girls talked about their imaginary herd of horses, which they referred to as their "dream herd." They developed their dream herd from watching Saturday morning TV with Trigger, Fury, Flicka and Silver, and from reading Walter Farley's Black Stallion books. They found that some of "their horses" were the same colors or had the same names as the TV horses. They could talk for hours about each one of them. They tended to their dream herd as they pulled tansy and ferns in the pasture.

On the long ride to and from the farm, the girls shared their big dreams of galloping stallions and herds of mares and foals. Lou's dad tried to talk realism to the girls, but their imagination and enthusiasm could not be curtailed. His plan to raise a few head of cattle did not impress the girls or sway them from their dream of horses. He eventually joined in the fun and teased them by spinning a yarn about "his most magnificent, powerful golden palomino stallion who was greater than any horse ever born and that was why he was buying a farm, as well as to raise cattle, of course." This was music to the girls' ears and impressed them very much. They pretended it was true and would beg him to show them his stallion. "Oh no," he would say, "Because he is so beautiful, his beauty would spoil any other horse you ever set eyes on." The girls rolled their eyes, and Lou's dad would chuckle.

Eventually summer came and school was out. The girls had both graduated from the eighth grade and Lou's family packed up to move to the farm. The parting was bittersweet for Lou and Kandee.

They would miss each other so much. They understood that their connection—the school bus—was gone. The farm was over 30 miles away and seeing each other would be difficult, but they planned to talk on the phone often and stay friends forever.

Kandee said, "I'll find a way to come visit you whenever I can. My mom just started a new job, so she won't mind. She knows how much I like going out to your farm. She even said she would try to share with transportation, if only one way. I know she is very busy and works some evenings. But it's summertime so I should be able to stay longer, if it's okay with your parents."

Lou said, "I'll try to get my folks to come pick you up every weekend." Lou knew this was wishful thinking because her mom worked in the city as a nurse with unpredictable hours and a long commute in the opposite direction. Lou's dad was a mechanic at the airport, working swing-shift with rotating days off. It seemed nearly impossible to figure out how they would get together. No buses traveled anywhere near the farm, but since Lou's folks liked Kandee very much and thought the girls got along so well, they were willing to pick her up, if the schedule was planned strategically.

After a couple of weeks of planning over the phone, the best they could do was to meet at a movie theater in a town part way between their homes. Kandee could ride the bus as far as it would go to a bus station that was near the movie theater. They had to plan their meetings carefully, to coincide with the picture show and Lou's parents' schedule for transportation.

Finally arrangements were made and they were so excited to see each other again. Just in case the theater was crowded, they decided to dress alike.

"Be sure to wear your red sweatshirt," one said.

"And a man's tie," the other added, "So we will recognize each other." It felt like forever since they had been together.

Kandee and Lou loved to spend time together. Their overnight stays were like slumber parties because they stayed awake talking and laughing long into the night. They planned elaborate adventures involving the horse they hoped to have soon. Lou's dad worked swing-shift, and by the time he came home he would find the girls still whispering and giggling.

"You girls get to sleep right now," he would scold. "It's very late and way past your bedtime. Besides, I'm tired and I don't want to hear any noise. Morning will be here too soon."

One late night as the girls were brushing their hair, Lou was feeling very frustrated because her parents didn't feel the urgency that Lou was feeling about getting a horse. Lou felt that, since they now had a farm they should get a horse, but Lou's dad seemed to keep busy doing everything, except putting an effort into looking for a horse.

"Why won't my folks just drop everything they are doing and let us find a horse?" Lou bemoaned to Kandee's sympathetic ear. "Dad always finds another project to work on. Mom is so busy and hardly ever home. She doesn't seem to care if we ever get a horse. It is so hard to wait; every day seems like years. Why do they always think everything is more important that getting a horse?"

She waved the hair brush in the air and continued to express her pent-up thoughts. "Before we moved here, I told my dad I was going to 'bust' if I didn't get a horse. He told me he didn't want me to 'bust', and he would do everything in his power to help me get one. Now everything is practically ready, but he makes no effort to actually *get a horse*. Why not? I don't understand parents!" Lou plopped down on the bed. "Why even get a farm if we don't get a horse?" Then with a gleam in her eye, she said, "Hey, maybe we should start riding Betsy! Barney is still too small to ride. If they see us riding the cow, maybe then they'd see how desperate we are and get us a horse!"

Kandee listened to Lou's ravings. Then she said, as she sat beside Lou on the bed, "Betsy probably won't like us to ride her, but it might be fun to try. It could make her hold back her milk though, which would upset your dad, and he might keep you waiting even longer to get a horse. A better idea might be for you to keep praying. I'll pray, too. Also, let's ask your dad what we can do to help get things more prepared for a horse, then maybe he won't have an excuse to wait any longer. I don't want you to 'bust' either," she added with a smile. They both giggled—and that become a long fit of laughter.

CHAPTER 1

LIFE ON THE FARM

The next Saturday morning, Lou and Kandee were helping Lou's mom make butter from the rich cream that Betsy gave them. The girls took turns shaking the quart jar that held the cream. It took a long time and a lot of shaking to turn the cream into butter. They would spend what seemed like hours just shaking the jar of cream. Their arms grew tired but they continued to take turns shaking the butter jar. It helped if music with a good rhythm was playing on the radio. Sometimes they would compete to see who could shake the jar the longest. Arms would ache, and what started as fun soon became a real chore. Once the butter was churned, they had to mash it with a fork to make sure all the buttermilk was separated. When Lou's mom was satisfied, they mashed in a small amount of salt. The first batch of butter tasted too salty, but with a little practice they got it just right. Lou's mom put the finished product into the freezer, which was becoming full.

Soon Lou's dad came into the house after milking Betsy again, with more milk in a bucket. Lou's mom took the fresh milk and strained it. She explained how the cream would separate from the milk after being allowed to chill overnight. "Tomorrow we can make more butter out of the cream that will rise," she stated.

Lou and Kandee groaned. "Oh no. Not more cream. Our arms are tired from this batch. Guess it's a good thing there are two of us to do this chore." The girls began to complain that their day was wasting because they had lots of plans. They always planned more activities than they could possibly do in a day.

Lou's dad exclaimed, "You girls are closer than sisters. Sisters fight sometimes, but you two never do."

"Well, if we are closer than sisters, I'll have to call you both Mom and Dad too," Kandee exclaimed. Lou's mom and dad beamed!

Mom said, "You girls are like two peas-in-a-pod; one blonde with blue eyes, and the other with a long ponytail and big brown eyes. Whenever I look at Betsy's eyes, I always think of you, Kandee."

"When you see my eyes, do I remind you of Betsy?" Kandee asked. The family all laughed, then Lou and Kandee headed out the door.

That evening, Dad told the girls that Betsy needed to be milked every morning and every evening. He could milk in the morning, but because he worked swing shift, he told Lou he was depending on her to milk Betsy in the evenings.

"I don't want her milk to dry up," Dad said.

Lou and Kandee looked sheepishly at each other, remembering how they had plotted to ride Betsy.

Lou liked Betsy and was willing to do this chore; however, Betsy did not like Lou to do the milking. Lou did not have a strong squeeze and Betsy would hold back her milk. Betsy wanted Dad to milk her.

Kandee tried her best to milk Betsy too, whenever she came to the farm. Dad continued to worry that Betsy would lose her milk, if she wasn't milked properly both morning and night.

One evening as Lou tried to milk Betsy, a neighbor boy came and sat on the section of fence that Lou's dad had recently completed. He held an accordion which he played very well. Lou yelled a "hello" to him, but he didn't answer. Lou continued to milk Betsy, who wouldn't stand still for her. When she finished, she noticed the boy had left without talking to her.

"That was a strange serenade," Lou thought.

A few nights later, as she was milking again, she noticed the boy on her lawn walking on his hands. "Wow, he is really coordinated," Lou marveled, "I have never been able to do that."

This time, he did not run off and actually came up to Betsy while Lou was milking. After watching a while, he said, "You know, you're not very good at that and your cow isn't very happy. That's why she stomps her feet and won't hold still."

"I know she doesn't like me. If you can do better, why don't you try?" Lou suggested.

The boy said "Okay, let me sit there, and I'll show you how it's done." He sat on the three-legged stool and rubbed Betsy's flank while talking soothingly to her, then proceeded to milk. He leaned his dark head against Betsy's flank. "By the way, my name is Brian."

"Hi, my name is Lou." She eyed Brian's milking technique. "Betsy really likes you," Lou noticed. "She likes my dad too. I don't think she likes me. Maybe she only likes men to milk her. Where did you learn to milk so well?"

Brian looked at Lou with his mischievous blue eyes. "We used to have cows too. I kind of miss them. I like the way they smell and love to drink their fresh warm milk." Laughing, he squirted Lou in the face with a stream of milk.

Lou licked the milk off of her mouth and wiped her face with her sleeve. "You can come help any evening if you want. My dad wouldn't mind. He works swing shift and he's worried that I'm not doing a good job milking in the evenings, and that might cause Betsy to dry up. She really doesn't like my technique."

"Maybe I will, whenever I can," Brian decided.

Lou told her dad about Brian's offer to help. Her dad wanted to meet him. On his next day off, rather than milk Betsy himself in the evening, he sent Lou out to do the job. Brian appeared shortly after and took over the milking. Lou's dad came out to meet this incredible young man. They liked each other immediately.

"Would you like the job of milking in the evenings when I'm at work?" Lou's dad asked Brian. "I'll pay you for your good milking skills. Lou told me Betsy likes your milking style."

"Sure," Brian replied. "I like cows. I do have a summer job at a chicken farm, but I'm home in the evenings."

"Do you like horses?" Lou asked wonderingly.

"Sure, I like horses too. I like all animals."

As time passed, Lou's family and Brian became good friends. Brian enjoyed discussing topics such as science and mechanics with Lou's dad, and together they often work on cars. Brian also helped with the ongoing project of building the fence. One day, after Brian had left, Lou's dad made the comment kiddingly, "Brian is a real nice person and a lot of help. I like that boy. Lou, I want that boy for a son-in-law."

Lou looked up in shock at her dad. She wrinkled her nose. "Dad, don't be silly,' she said with a frown. "When are we going to get a horse? That's all I want."

Lou's mom had little time to devote to farm life because of her busy work schedule. She asked the girls to pitch in and help with the housework. Each day she would leave a list of projects she wanted Lou to do. She knew Kandee was always willing to help too, and somehow, the results were better when Kandee was there. Usually the girls had to clean house, picking up newspapers in the living room, dusting, vacuuming, and tidying everything, as well as washing dishes and cleaning Lou's room, which always seemed to be messy. Weekly, they did the laundry and scrubbed out the bathtub.

Sometimes, Dad would sit in the living room, slowly reading—then dropping the newspaper page by page onto the floor. The girls dusted and vacuumed around him, wishing he would hurry and finish. He dawdled because he liked to tease them and he enjoyed being the center of their attention. They would fluff the pillow under his head and put his feet on the foot stool as they questioned how his magnificent powerful golden palomino stallion was doing, hoping to engage Dad in a conversation about his imaginary horse. He enjoyed watching them become exasperated, as he avoided their horse questions and pointed out every little problem he could find such as a speck of dust or wrinkle in the sofa cover, and always his soft chuckle would follow them as they left the room.

The girls were also expected to make Dad's lunch and pack his lunchbox to take to work. Lou was not allowed to "play" until the work was done. Many days, the girls couldn't wait until Dad left for work mid-afternoon, because they had freedom until Mom came home in the evening, and then it was time to get Betsy in for milking. They always made the most of those "free" hours. There was never a dull moment then. They picked berries by the handfuls and ate them in the neighboring berry fields; they explored the woods behind the house, listened to Lou's transistor radio, tended their "dream herd" and planned the adventures they would have with the real horse, *IF* they ever got one.

5

CHAPTER 2

THE DREAM COMES TRUE!

One miraculous day in July, Lou called Kandee with the news, "*I have a horse!!!*"

Kandee was just as excited as Lou sounded! Lou described her new horse, a three-year old bay Morgan/Thoroughbred gelding.

"He is golden-red with a black mane and tail, with silver legs that turn to black near his hooves, and he has a few specks of white hairs on his neck, and his underside is a creamy tan color. He actually glows all over!" Lou said as she ran out of breath.

Kandee couldn't imagine such a magnificent looking horse. She couldn't wait to see him! "Tell me everything right from the beginning, please don't leave out anything, no matter how small! I want to hear about it all, as if I were there too!" Kandee said excitedly, as she stretched out the phone cord to slide down the wall and sit on the floor.

Lou explained how she had obtained this wonderful horse. Dad had taken her to a livestock auction under the pretense of looking for a pump for the well.

Lou continued, "I didn't want to go, but then Dad said there might be livestock there. I was so excited that I ran to the truck and yelled for Dad to hurry up. He seemed to take forever, and then was laughing at me as he slid behind the steering wheel. Finally we were on our way."

Before the auction started, Lou had dragged her dad behind the auction building to look for the horses. They wound around through pens of cows, sheep, goats, and pigs. Lou found it hard not to run, but was slowed down by the pull on her dad's hand. Beyond the pens, horse trailers were lined up and horses were tied to the sides of the trailers. Lou pulled harder on her dad's hand. "Come on Dad, faster," she pleaded.

There were all kinds of horses, large and small, black and white, some pacing back and forth, some nickering to each other. Lou's eyes opened wide in all the wonder. Her heart was beating fast and she felt her wish for a horse leap in her heart. She stood still and searched with her eyes, taking them all in. One horse, a beautiful bay, tossed his head and stood watching her intently, as if he was waiting for her. He didn't move a muscle as Lou approached him with her palms up and arms stretched out in front of her. Then he nickered softly and nuzzled each hand. Lou's arms had a mind of their own as they wrapped around his neck. She felt his silky mane fall over her hair as she breathed in his wonderful "horse scent". She tucked her own hair behind her ears, to feel closer to him.

The horse's owner said, "Hey girl, you look like you need a horse."

Lou's eyes were big and round as she agreed wholeheartedly that she did need a horse, and the bay's owner asked permission to lift Lou onto his bare back. "If you buy him, I'll include his tack: this leather bridle, halter and lead rope; no saddle though, sorry." he said.

Lou sat on this magnificent horse as if she were in a dream. This was real? It did not feel real. She realized this was a very important moment in her life and whispered, "What's his name?"

"Flash," the man said.

The name sounded like musical magic to Lou's ears. Flash, Lou thought, *Flash*. I love it. It's a perfect name. I love him.

"Go on, ride around a bit and see what you think of him," Lou's dad encouraged.

Lou couldn't believe it! She didn't ride a horse, she floated on a cloud! Flash flicked his ears back and forth and arched his neck, patiently waiting for the signal to go.

As they walked through the crowds, people she encountered said, "Nice horse." Some said, "I'll trade you." Others said, "Want to sell him?"

"No way," Lou flared. Flash danced sideways and tossed his head. He was the best horse any girl ever rode, the best horse in the world, the best horse ever born. She was in heaven. She had to have *this* horse! She let Flash pick up the pace. He flicked his ears back and forth again, moving into an easy trot. Flash snorted and stretched out his neck, wanting to move faster. He seemed to like this young person on his back. They reached the end of the grounds, where Lou reluctantly turned Flash around to go back to his owner and her dad.

Lou was elated, but afraid that she would have to get off, give up Flash, and never see him again. But to her astonishment, her dad said, "How do you like him?" as if he couldn't tell from Lou's rapturous expression.

Her blonde hair had come out from behind her ears and fell across her shoulders, her eyes sparkled with happiness. Lou said, "I love him. He's perfect. He's the one I've always been dreaming of. Please can we get him?" She held her breath and whispered a prayer, afraid of the answer.

Dad said, "I just bought him. Flash's owner will haul him home for us. You've got yourself a horse."

Lou exhaled with tears in her eyes, a prayer of thanks on her lips, and joy in her heart. She had her horse, a big beautiful bay! Flash tossed his head and snorted, as if to give his own stamp of approval to his new owner. With a sigh, Lou slid from his back and gave him a big kiss on the downy softness between his nostrils. She gave him a big hug around his neck. Her dream had come true.

CHAPTER 3

OWNERSHIP

That first night home, Lou was told she needed to keep Flash staked out on a rope, since the fencing was not quite finished.

Lou wanted to sleep outside in a sleeping bag near Flash, but her parents said no. It was hard for Lou to go inside. She rechecked his halter and stake-out rope, and added some hay and fresh water for him. She wrapped her arms around his neck and talked to him quietly, "I'll see you in the morning. Be a good boy and stay safe. Good night." Flash flicked his ears and lowered his head, searching her hands for treats. He enjoyed all this attention.

That night Flash got tangled in the rope, and had a bad rope burn under his fetlock above his right hind hoof. When Lou ran outside to see him first thing in the morning, he stood with his head down and his hind foot up. Lou was heartsick.

Lou's mom was running late for work, but took the time to collect the medical supplies needed to tend the wound. She put the supplies in a bucket and handed it to Lou. As she was heading out the door, she quickly explained how to care for a wound such as Flash's rope burn. As Mom drove down the driveway, she said to Lou, "It's a big job, but I know you can do it." Lou was on her own with his care.

Lou tucked her blonde hair behind her ears and with tears in her eyes, she began to tend to Flash's wound, washing it gently. Flash did not want her to touch his sore and he would pick up his foot and set it down. He kept flicking his tail in Lou's face. That stung! His tail kept getting in the way of tending the wound, causing her to have to start the wrapping process over and over. One more swish of Flash's tail stung her face again! Lou reached her wit's end, and she decided to fix this problem. She took the scissors in one hand and Flash's tail in the other, then cut off the tail above his hocks. It's short; I do like his tail longer, but it'll grow back. This will make caring for him easier, she thought.

Lou was determined and after several tries, she was able to wrap his foot, but was not sure how long the poorly applied bandage would stay on. She needed another pair of hands.

When Lou finished dressing the wound, she picked up the shiny black cut tail in her hands. This is too beautiful to throw away, she thought, as she wrapped twine tightly around the top. I think I'll hang this in my room. When she finished caring for Flash, she put her medical supplies back into the bucket and went into the house to call Kandee. After telling her everything, she asked Kandee to come help with doctoring Flash and with painting the wooden fence.

"With both of us here, I'm sure my folks will let us sleep outside with Flash," Lou said. "I can't let him get hurt again. I'm going to start painting the fence boards now. We have to get this fence finished!"

Kandee persuaded her mother to take her to Lou's house that night. Lou's parents allowed the two girls to sleep outside next to the staked-out horse, to keep an eye on him so he didn't injure himself again. The girls slept out under the stars for several nights.

Kandee held Flash while Lou administered the medical care he needed. She would whisper into his ear, rub his neck, play with his warm soft muzzle and tickle him behind his ears; anything she could do to keep his attention while Lou cleaned, applied medicine, and wrapped his foot. They found that working together finished the job quickly and Flash soon learned to hold his foot still. Lou was happy to have her extra pair of hands.

All the work became fun for the girls, especially when Flash showed signs of healing. They would talk, laugh and make plans for riding as they painted the fence boards, while Flash munched grass in the background.

"By the way," Kandee said, "Flash does not look anything like your description of him. You described him in so much detail and in so many little sections, I couldn't put it all together in my mind. But you are right, he does actually glow, and he is even more magnificent than I could imagine!"

So the girls took care of Flash and painted the fence. When he could, Dad was out there working too. After the boards dried, he would take them and attach them to the posts. Soon the white board fence enclosed the small farm; it was beautiful!

Flash nickered each time the girls came near. They brought him treats and would talk to him as if he were another person. He always watched for them and was developing a strong bond. He checked Lou's hands and pockets, then would go to Kandee and search her. He was tired of being tied up. Now that the fence was finished, they set him free to run in the field. Before long, he was well enough to ride.

Lou and Kandee rode him every free moment of the day. They rode bareback because they didn't have a saddle. At first, it was hard for them to mount Flash. Kandee could give Lou a lift up, but for

Kandee to mount behind Lou they needed something to climb on. They would look for a stump, a rock, a hillside—anything they could find to give Kandee a boost.

Finally, after much practicing, Lou learned to grab Flash's mane in both hands, then spring up and wiggle her body onto his back. When Kandee next visited she was amazed that Lou could jump so well, especially since she couldn't jump very high.

The girls practiced mounting double, but sometimes Kandee pulled Lou off with her attempts to mount. The girls would laugh so hard, they would have to give up trying until they gained control of their giggles. Flash would stand and wait patiently for them to get on him. Eventually, they both learned how to mount. Lou mounted first, then they would hold onto each other's arm above the elbows, and Kandee would make a running leap while Lou used her left leg to push Kandee up behind her.

It wasn't long before they learned how to balance themselves without relying on each other. If one began to lose her balance, she could adjust without unbalancing the other one. They would take off at a gallop, adjusting their positions as needed. Sometimes, after a quick stop, Lou would end up on Flash's withers, and then in unison both girls would scoot back.

Sometimes they would ride to the river and take Flash out for a swim. Flash liked the water and they would cling to his mane as he swam. Kandee would be on one side and Lou would be on the other side, both avoiding his swirling legs. After a good swim, they would wander through the berry fields eating fresh raspberries along the way. Flash learned to avoid the thorns and delicately pick his own berries from the bushes. Sometimes Flash would wait for Lou and Kandee to pick a handful for him. He acted as if the berries tasted better when the girls hand-fed him.

The two girls and one horse soon became a well-known sight everywhere they rode throughout the countryside. They were a unique team.

CHAPTER 4

HORSE TRAINERS

One day the girls set up a jump to see if Flash could be a jumper. Dad watched as he sat on the porch of the house, shaking his head at their efforts. Flash was not being very cooperative unless, however, the jump was directed towards the old shed used as a barn. Then Flash would take every jump as if he was born to it, then run all the way and stop at the barn door.

Dad chuckled as he exclaimed, "By the way, that horse has you both trained, not vice versa."

Flash had a lot of tolerance for his two riders who were trainers-in-training. However, Dad decided that maybe the girls needed some sound knowledge about what they were trying to do.

The next day, with a big smile, he presented the girls with a brown paper bag. "Here, this is for you, to teach you what you are trying to teach to your horse. Somebody needs to know what they are doing," he stated.

The girls opened the bag and found a book on training horses from basic riding to fancy tricks. They were so pleased that Dad could be so thoughtful. They couldn't wait to get started.

Dad said, "You better read that book before working with Flash again. I don't want to waste my money, or have you girls get hurt."

Lou and Kandee eagerly ran to Lou's room to start studying to be horse trainers. While Lou was browsing through the book, Kandee noticed the horse tail hanging on the wall. "Hey, I like your wall hanging," she said.

Lou glanced up and said, "Yes. It was too pretty to throw away. I really like it too. I feel as if I have Flash here in my room."

"That tail is better than a picture. You should keep it forever," Kandee said.

The next day, they practiced the training program that they had spent the whole night reading about.

Before long, the girls had a training routine that Flash understood. Then they decided to play games with him. They put him through an obstacle course. Sometimes, Lou would cling to him like a monkey as they practiced pole-bending around Mom's newly planted apple trees. Other times, they practiced circus acts, taking turns standing or lying on Flash, while he was being led. Sometimes Lou would cling with one leg while reaching down at a gallop to pick up an object from the ground.

Another game was hide-and-seek from Flash, when the girls climbed trees with his oat bucket to see if he could find them. When he did, Lou would leap carefully out of the tree onto his back, but he stood still waiting for his oats. He made sure the girls knew how to play this game his way.

Flash had the patience of a saint. He let the girls climb under him, over him, and around him. He even allowed them to hook their bare toes over his hocks and pull his tail to mount over his rump.

Lou decided Flash was so smart, he needed to learn some of the tricks she read about in the book. He soon learned to kiss her under the chin, shake hands, nod yes when she asked if he loved her, and bow with one knee on the ground. Sometimes Flash would bow and let Lou mount from the bowed position. Lou was sure she had the smartest horse ever born.

Flash's favorite activity was to eat grass. He often had to do this with the girls sitting backwards on his back as they read books or listened to their transistor radio.

Flash tolerated everything these girls asked of him as long as food was his reward.

CHAPTER 5

FLASHING ARROW

One hot, sunny day as the girls were riding along the side of a dusty un-harvested hay field near Lou's home, a neighbor boy rode his horse up to them. The girls had not met this boy or this paint horse yet.

"You have a nice horse," Lou said to the boy.

He told them, "My horse is a race horse. Betcha a million dollars my horse can out-run your horse. Your horse is just a nag."

The girls puffed up like mad roosters at these words.

The boy said his horse was a registered champion Quarter Horse, who had won many races. The paint horse did look as if he had just stepped out of a magazine. The boy sat in a beautiful black saddle. He wore polished cowboy boots and a fancy black cowboy hat.

The girls rode bareback in cut-off jeans. They were barefoot. But those were fighting words. No one calls their magnificent steed a nag!

"Bet Flash can beat your horse with both of us riding him," Lou retorted.

"Wanna race?" the neighbor boy taunted. "Bet you'll lose."

"Bet we won't!" Kandee insisted.

As the kids lined up their horses, Lou wrapped her hands firmly in Flash's mane, and Kandee reached around Lou with one hand and did the same. Her other hand firmly gripped Lou's waist. Flash tossed his head and pawed the ground. They counted to three, then took off in a mad dash. Flash, with Lou and Kandee clinging to him, flew like the wind! Flash laid his ears back and took the lead immediately. The girls felt the sting of the tall grass slap against their bare legs. Flash's sweat soon made it difficult to keep their grip on his slippery body, but they hunkered down, hung on, and encouraged Flash to run even faster. Flash's feet pounded the dirt and he raced like never before. The boy and his horse did not pass them.

At the end of the field, the girls reined Flash in and looked behind them. The boy had turned his horse around and was about half-way back to the start. He was laughing very hard.

"Fooled you," he yelled. "You silly girls think I'm going to let my horse get winded in this dusty field? Forget it!" He rode off in the opposite direction.

Lou and Kandee climbed off of Flash, who stood with his head down and sides heaving.

"That dumb boy!" Lou said.

"What a great ride," Kandee said, as she patted Flash lovingly.

"We better just walk Flash the rest of the way home, to cool him down and give him a rest," Lou suggested, as she rubbed the sweat from Flash's face.

The girls contemplated the "race" as they walked with Flash trailing; his head between their shoulders and his hard breathing beginning to slow. They took turns patting him lovingly. He seemed glad for the restful walk.

"Flash would have won; he ran so fast." Kandee said. "He didn't eat any dust. That was a beautiful horse, but too pretty to get dirty. How can you have fun with a horse like that?"

Lou said, "Yep, I know. But we should shine Flash up like that sometime. He'd be just as beautiful, and he really is fast, as fast as a flashing arrow. Hey, I think that will be Flash's full name, *Flashing Arrow*. He earned it. We will still call him Flash for short, though."

Lou started humming a song. She had been thinking of a song for Flash for a while; now the words poured out of her.

> **"Flash, Flash, Flashing Arrow**
> **Racing over the plains,**
> **Flash, Flash, Flashing Arrow**
> **With your flying tail and mane.**
> **I'm as happy as can be,**
> **You're the only horse for me.**
> **Flash, Flash, Flashing Arrow**
> **My great horse, my own."**

"Just let any dumb boy think he can win a race against Flashing Arrow. No way!" Lou added.

So the girls in their bare feet and with their tired and dirty but magnificent race horse, *Flashing Arrow*, walked the rest of the way home.

CHAPTER 6

MYSTIC PHANTOM

Kandee loved Flash and was grateful to ride him, but that didn't keep her from wanting a horse of her own. She couldn't quit dreaming of having a horse.

"We could have even more fun, if I had a horse too," she told Lou. Lou agreed, but neither girl could figure out how to make that happen. They had enough trouble just getting together.

The girls planned to ride Flash almost every day. Usually the changeable weather did not discourage them from riding, but one day was exceptionally gray and rainy. The girls stayed indoors looking out the window at the downpour and gloom.

"The weather is so terrible! Why won't this rain let up?" they wailed.

Late in the day the rain subsided, but the clouds were low and visibility was terrible.

"We don't care about the fog. The rain has let up. Let's ride anyway," Kandee suggested.

The girls decided to ride close to the road rather than through the muddy berry fields because the fog was denser than they realized. This was a different way than they usually rode, but they thought their regular route might be too muddy after so much rain.

"We'll follow the road until we get past the little creek, then we can cut across to the berry field on the hill. Maybe it won't be so muddy there," Lou suggested.

After crossing the creek, they neared a stone house next to a small pasture. Flash snorted when Lou asked him to turn towards the berry fields. He side stepped and pointed his nose toward the pasture. Lou let him have his way. Flash took them along the side of the small pasture which was mostly covered with blackberry vines. The girls knew they were following a fence line, but they couldn't see the fence because the fog was thick and mist from the ground was creeping up to meet the fog. Flash moved slowly and deliberately along the fence line, then suddenly stood very still, tossing his head and pointing his ears forward with curiosity. He snorted. Close by a twig snapped, then another, followed by total silence, except for rain drops falling from some nearby trees.

Lou whispered, "What was that sound?"

Kandee answered in a quiet tone, "Maybe a deer?"

Then they heard more snapping of branches and berry vines. Flash side stepped closer to the fence and Lou urged him forward into an open space. The fog was so thick it was impossible to see anything.

They could barely make out a group of small trees overgrown with wild blackberries on a hill. They heard the sound again, coming from those trees.

"I wonder what is making that sound?" asked Kandee.

Lou added, "Flash wants to see what it is, too. He's not afraid of whatever is making the sound, so it is probably nothing we should be scared of."

The girls heard another snap of a branch, then a series of crunches and more snaps, then again silence. Flash nickered softly. The girls saw movement and wondered aloud what it could be. Lou and Kandee, who were riding bareback as always, felt a shiver run through Flash's body as he softly nickered a greeting. The girls starred into the fog and suddenly as the fog thinned briefly, a beautiful white horse appeared. He just stood on the hill with the fog swirling around him. He was as curious about Flash as Flash was about him. The girls were taking in all the beauty of the moment, seeing a dream, or was it an apparition? They continued to stare. Flash whinnied, and this time there was an answer from this magical horse. The white horse was not an apparition; he was beautiful and real. He came close to the fence and sniffed noses with Flash.

Kandee was mesmerized. She dismounted and reached over the rickety fence to pet the white horse. The girls didn't even notice it had begun to rain again.

"Where did you come from?" Kandee asked the white horse, as they picked the blackberries and fed them to the new horse. This new horse liked the berries and soon became very friendly. They noticed the horse was soaking wet and quite muddy. He had a smaller, more refined build than Flash. Kandee wondered if he could be an Arabian.

"Don't you have any shelter?" Kandee asked.

"Hey, what are you girls doing?" A man yelled at them from the stone house. He started toward the field pulling on his coat as he walked. The girls were too close and too scared to run. They introduced themselves and told the man that Flash found this horse and they were just making friends.

The old man could tell the girls meant no harm. In a strong accent, he introduced himself as Mr. Tony. He said he lived alone and was taking care of the horse for some friends who lived at the beach.

He said, "The owners would not like anyone to mess with this horse."

Lou and Kandee assured him that they would never do anything to hurt the horse; that they could tell he was lonely, so they were giving him love and attention. They continued to rub and pet the white horse.

The girls asked, "What is the horse's name?"

Mr. Tony said in his thick accent, "I don't even know. I just call him Whitey."

That evening the girl's discussed "Whitey." The girls thought that was a terrible name for such a beautiful and magnificent horse. As they sat on the back porch thinking of him, they wrote on the porch's blackboard trying out various spellings of wonderful sounding names. They finally decided to call him *Mystic Phantom*, because he really seemed like a phantom coming out of the mist.

Visiting Mystic Phantom became the girls' favorite destination. After several visits, Mr. Tony told the girls he could use some help picking berries, if the girls would be interested in a job. Lou and Kandee were excited, but they said they would have to ask their parents.

"If we had a job, we could afford horse shoes for Flash and we can come see Mystic Phantom every day!"

Lou's mom went to meet Mr. Tony, and then checked with Kandee's mom, who seemed pleased that Kandee would have a job and be able to spend more time in the country, as she was so busy with her own new job. Lou's mom assured Kandee's mom both girls would save their earnings. The girls were happy they could spend the whole berry season together! Kandee was secretly thrilled to be near Mystic Phantom all day.

Each day, after picking berries from sun up to mid-afternoon, they would go home to get Flash and ride back over to spend time with Mystic Phantom. Mr. Tony grew more confident that the girls knew how to handle themselves around the horse. He was glad to see the neglected horse get some attention. The girls groomed Mystic every day and he finally looked like the magnificent, shiny, white horse the girls envisioned him to be. Mr. Tony let the girls feed the horse and muck out the enclosure. They even cleared away the overgrown wild blackberry vines to make the enclosure larger for Mystic. Mr. Tony liked their help. He was glad he didn't have to do all this work himself.

The girls rigged up a rope halter and rode Mystic in his small enclosure. They could tell he was well trained.

"Mystic needs some exercise. He doesn't have room to run in here," Kandee exclaimed. "Can we take him out of this little field and ride through your berry field to give him some exercise?" she asked Mr. Tony.

Mr. Tony agreed and said, "Make this a brief ride. I am nervous that something might happen to the white horse. His owners will be very upset if anything happens to him."

Mr. Tony soon learned the horse was in good hands with the girls. A few days later he told the girls, "I talked to this horse's owners last night and told them how much help and good care you are giving him. I also told them what good riders you are. The owners appreciate your help and have given their permission to let you ride him. They are happy he is getting exercise, and they trust my judgment."

Kandee and Lou were ecstatic! Another horse, at last!

At the end of each work day, the girls, each with her own magnificent steed, rode through the berry fields. They would lose track of time and go for longer and longer rides.

Kandee exclaimed, "I think Mystic would do better if I had a bridle for him. He tends to get a little head strong at times." But, for now the homemade halter was all that was available for them to use.

One night they barely got back before dark. Mr. Tony came out to see them but did not get mad.

He said, "I need to be gone for a few days. There will be no berry-picking work for you until I return. You should have plenty of free time, so how would you girls like to take care of the white horse for me while I'm gone?"

Kandee and Lou were excited. "I'm sure we can do it, but we better ask my folks," Lou said.

Mom said, "If you girls take care of this horse, you need to bring him here. I'm not going to be responsible for a horse somewhere else."

Kandee and Lou's enthusiasm could not be curtailed! They planned their next day's ride as they rode double on Flash back over to Mr. Tony's, to get Mystic and bring him home with them.

CHAPTER 7

RIDING ADVENTURES

Having two horses was an almost unbelievable joy for the two girls. They could hardly decide where to ride first.

"We need to explore the new freeway that is being built," Lou suggested. "It is still just dirt. I know of one section that is not being worked on about four miles from here. I've been wanting to check it out."

The girls rode to the new freeway; then they rode along the dirt area that was to become the freeway. It stretched for miles. The girls wished the road workers would leave it like this, a nice, wide dirt riding path. They decided to race.

Flash and Mystic could feel the excitement! The horses knew something was going to happen. They liked the feel of the soft but firm dirt under their feet. Flash, arched his neck and danced sideways, as he tossed his head asking for more rein. His thick black mane was bouncing up and down with his movements. Mystic's tail was up like a white flag flowing in the breeze. He took little prancing steps and his ears were pricked forward. He shook his head from side to side. Kandee could feel the homemade halter was not doing much to control his prancing.

Lou said, "Mystic looks just like a picture!"

"I was going to say the same thing about Flash," Kandee said with a big smile on her face. "He is so beautiful! But this halter isn't working well," she added over her shoulder as Mystic lunged forward. "Let's try to work up to speed to see how he'll respond. You might have to come to my rescue," she added, this time with a grimace.

"Anytime," Lou replied with a laugh.

They planned to start slow, then work up to a gallop, then maybe an all-out run. As they started off, Lou noticed how Kandee's long ponytail, high up on her head, was moving in unison to the movements of Mystic's tail. This brought a grin to her face and put a sparkle in her blue eyes. Flash quickly returned her to reality. Lou tried to hold Flash back to give Mystic the lead. With a mind of his own, Flashed leaped forward, pulling Lou up on his withers, his black mane covering her face and getting into her eyes. She got back in place as he leaped again, tossing his head up and down, pushing his nose out to get more freedom. He wanted to run and not be held back. He had to catch Mystic!

Mystic had taken off and nothing could hold him back. He had the freedom—no bit to control his actions. His tail was flying high and his mane streamed out flicking Kandee in the face as he started gathering speed. His white body moved quickly along the dirt roadway. He could hear Flash's hoof beats coming closer. Flash moved alongside Mystic. The two horses, with each girl riding bareback, matched each other stride for stride. They were a sight to see! The girls' hair was blown away from their faces by the wind, as were the manes and tails of the horses, one a beautiful bay and the other a glimmering white. The girls' bodies moved with the rhythm of the muscled backs of their steeds.

Lou and Kandee turned their heads towards each other; their eyes streaming with tears from the wind. They grinned, and then laughed. After all those years of pretending with their dream herd—Trigger, Silver, Fury, Flicka and the Black Stallion, their dream was actually happening. This was real! This was a moment they would never forget.

Lou shifted her position on Flash's back giving him the signal to slow. Flash slowed down significantly. Kandee did the same with Mystic, but he had become competitive and pushed his nose out to run faster. He wasn't going to obey the pull on his halter. Kandee tried to turn Mystic, but he ignored her. She tried to lean further back, still no response. Mystic ran on.

Lou could tell Kandee was having trouble controlling Mystic, so she signaled Flash to speed up. He leaped forward, and soon matched Mystic stride for stride. They ran together, then at Lou's urging, Flash moved ahead turning his body towards Mystic, to slow him down. Lou reached over and grabbed Mystic's rope reins. He still did not want to stop, but with Lou and Flash's help, they moved him in a circle and were able to bring him to a halt. Mystic shook his head and Lou released the reins. Flash snorted and danced away. Mystic tossed his head again as Kandee slid off his back. He nuzzled her chest. Lou joined Kandee on the ground. Flash rubbed his sweaty head on her back, pushing her forward.

"Wow, what a ride!" Lou exclaimed.

"You're right, that was the best of rides! I don't ever want to forget it. Flash, you were the best!" Kandee hugged him. "Thanks for the rescue, Lou. You and Flash were really amazing!" She turned towards Mystic and smiled as she gave him a hug, too. Kandee was worried.

"I think I need a real bridle for Mystic. He doesn't listen to me when he's that excited."

The girls did not want anything to spoil their riding fun. They resolved to get a bridle somehow.

The next day their prayers were answered. While riding along the edge of a plowed field near an orchard, Kandee noticed what appeared to be a pile of mangled leather. The girls dismounted to investigate. Kandee pulled a straight bit from the disintegrated pile of leather straps. The mangled leather was hard and unusable.

"Hey, here's a metal bit," she exclaimed. "We can use this! Let's try to make a bridle for Mystic. After that race yesterday, I think he needs a bit in his mouth to help him respond better."

The girls rode the horses home to work on a bridle. By braiding baling twine and copying the design of Flash's bridle, the girls fashioned a fairly well-fitting bridle for Mystic. He did seem more responsive with it.

The girls continued riding the horses all over the countryside. They raced the horses occasionally, and the bit worked well.

Since the girls now had two horses to ride, Brian would come over to go riding with them. Sometimes his friend, Knoll, would come too. Brian was a good rider, probably because he was so agile. Knoll rode behind Kandee with his long legs almost reaching the ground on either side of Mystic.

One day they were all riding along maintenance roads under the power lines. The horses liked to gallop up the short, steep hills. One steep hill was covered with tall thistles and the horses galloped extra fast to get through the stickers and thistles. Lou felt Brian loosen his grip. He tumbled off and over Flash's rump, did a flip and landed on his feet. Lou, Kandee and Knoll were amazed at Brian's agility and were glad he was not hurt. Brian picked his way through the thistles to the top of the hill. He had collected a few stickers, and he stopped to pull them out before remounting Flash behind Lou.

The two horses and four riders enjoyed exploring the countryside. Both horses usually behaved perfectly and Flash and Mystic acted like best friends.

CHAPTER 8

THE GHOSTLY RIDE

That night, the girls were wide awake late, as usual. The moon was full and the night was bright. They heard Dad come home from work, so they tried to be quiet, but they were not tired. They were so excited to know two horses were waiting for them outside in the pasture. They decided to sneak out for a moonlight ride.

"It is a bright night, but a little chilly," Lou exclaimed as they headed out the door. Rather than go back to Lou's room to get their own coats, they decided to grab Dad's nice warm work coats from the hooks on the back porch. He had one older coat and one new work coat. The girls really liked riding in these large, warm coats, but Dad forbade the girls from using them, because the coats always came back dirty.

"You wear the new coat and I'll wear his old coat, but we better make sure we keep them clean. If the new coat gets dirty Dad will go easier on you than me, so you wear it," Lou said. They both smiled.

Kandee said, "Oh, I see how it is. If I'm the one to blame for getting his new coat dirty, he won't ground you from riding Flash." They slipped into the coats and quietly laughed as they left the porch.

Since there was no traffic this time of night, they decided to ride into the nearby town, a few miles away. The moon gave the countryside a translucent, surreal appearance. Mystic, being white, glowed like a phantom. Flash, being a dark horse, blended into the night as a shadow.

As the girls rode, the temperature grew colder and mist began to creep up from the ground.

The girls rode through the center of town. The town was so quiet. It appeared to be a ghost town. The only sound they heard was the footfall of the horses' hooves. This tone sounded strange as it seemed to reverberate down the road and off the buildings as they passed.

"This seems eerie. It is so quiet. Usually this is a hustling, bustling town," Lou said. Even their whispers seemed to have an echo, an odd sound. Lou felt an unusual chill and goose bumps. "This feels weird. Let's turn around. I keep remembering that creepy movie we watched and those stories that Brian was teasing us about."

"Me too," Kandee said, "I know they were just stories, but I feel as if we are being watched."

"Yeah," Lou said, "we better head home. I don't like it so quiet and—ghostly. It's almost scary! I feel like running all the way home."

Even the horses appeared nervous and spooky to be out this time of night. They tossed their heads and side-stepped frequently. They rode home quickly. The only sounds the girls heard were the horses' hoof-beats which seemed to have an unworldly echo; an unusual sound which the girls had never noticed before. The girls looked behind themselves and all round in the gloomy darkness to make sure no ghost or boogey-man was coming after them as they rode home as quickly as they could possibly go.

When they arrived home, they felt very relieved to have made it home safely. They put the horses in the pasture. They hung Dad's coats back on the same hooks hoping the coats had stayed clean, but they really couldn't tell in the dark. Then they crawled back in bed. They slept very soundly the rest of the night and into the morning. When they awoke, their scary moonlight ride felt like a dream.

The girls were very happy having two horses to ride. These were the best few days of Kandee's life.

"I just have to try to buy Mystic," she told Lou. I just don't know where I'd keep him, though."

Lou offered to keep him for Kandee, if Kandee persuaded her mother to buy him. "I'm sure my folks won't mind," Lou said, "but we should let them know what we want to do."

"Thanks, but your place won't be close enough to me. I would want to see him and take care of him all the time," Kandee stated dejectedly, "but it might work for a while until I can find a place to keep him near my home."

When Mr. Tony returned from his trip, he was pleased to see the white horse had been well cared for. He gave the girls the freedom to ride Mystic whenever and wherever they wanted, after the berries had been picked, of course.

Kandee and Lou lost track of time. This summer was the most wonderful time. It seemed as if it would never end. Even though summer was not over, raspberry-picking season did end and Kandee's mom wanted her to come home.

CHAPTER 9

RUN AWAY FROM HOME

The girls talked on the phone as often as they could over the next few days. Kandee missed Mystic very much. Lou went to check on him frequently and reported back to Kandee.

"Mystic misses you too. He acts like he wants to jump the fence and ride alongside Flash," Lou told her after a recent visit.

"I miss him so much," sighed Kandee.

"We need to take the horses and run away from home," Lou suggested.

Kandee thought that was a good idea. They started making their plans.

"If we camp near the river, we will have plenty of water for the horses," Lou said.

"If we find a grassy spot, we can stake them out so they can get plenty to eat," Kandee said. "We can pack some oats too."

"We'll have to take turns sleeping, so we can keep an eye on them. I don't want Flash to get another rope burn," Lou mentioned.

The next time Kandee came to stay for a few days, they put their plans into action. They packed sleeping bags and food. They took matches to build a fire. They packed a change of clothes and towels.

When they were all packed up, they found they had too much stuff to carry bareback on the horses, so they had to pare down their supplies. The change of clothes and towels got left behind.

Finally they were ready to go, and they planned to leave in the morning.

That night, Dad called them into his room. He had overheard them making their plans.

"Okay," he said, "I know you two are planning to run away from home. I'm not trying to stop you, but you have to tell me where you are going or else you're grounded from riding horses."

Lou and Kandee were crestfallen. It wouldn't be the same adventure if the parents knew where they were going, but they surely didn't want to go without the horses. They told dad their plans.

He said, "Okay, now I know how to find you in case of emergency. Go ahead and run away from home. Be back by suppertime tomorrow."

Lou and Kandee looked at each other. Oh no, they had a time limit! Well, they just would have to go have a really good time really fast.

They went to tell Mr. Tony that Mystic would be gone overnight. Mr. Tony had no objection. He was glad to see the girls and he knew Mystic had missed being ridden. He was glad the horse would get attention again. He told them to ride safely. They assured him that they would.

"We'll have him back by supper tomorrow," they said as they waved good-bye.

The girls and their trusty steeds made it down to the river. They searched until they found a nice grassy meadow where they decided to make their camp. They staked out the horses who began to nibble the grass.

The girls then began to set up their own camp. They decided to light a fire to heat some soup for supper. However, they had forgotten paper to start a fire. They tried twigs and leaves, but everything near the river was slightly damp. They used all the matches, but couldn't get a fire going.

"Well, we'll just eat our soup cold," Lou said.

They discovered another problem. They had forgotten a can opener.

"There has to be a way to open this can," Kandee said. They used a knife and pounded it with a rock. Success finally! They got the lid off. The girls ate cold soup ravenously from the can.

After dinner, the girls decided to take an exploratory ride before crawling into their sleeping bags.

"We should make sure there are no bears or other wild critters around," Lou said.

They rode the horses through the woods along the river and checked for signs of other animals.

"Everything seems to be okay," Kandee acknowledged.

Kandee had been humming to Mystic as they rode. She knew she couldn't carry a tune to sing like Lou did about Flash. Since she had some Native American heritage, she decided to chant. Before long, Mystic's rhythm and Kandee's words blended together and she decided to chant it out loud:

> **"Mystic Phantom, a white, white horse.**
> **Mystic Phantom I love you of course**
> **'Cuz you're a dream in one of my schemes.**
> **Mystic Phantom you run so fast**
> **Side by side with dear ol' Flash**
> **With an arch in your neck and your tail flying high.**
> **You make people sigh just to see you go by.**
> **Mystic Phantom, a dream horse.**
> **Mystic Phantom I love you of course."**

"That's great," Lou exclaimed. "I really like it. Mystic seems to like it, too. He knows you're talking about him."

Soon the girls went back to their cold camp to prepare to sleep. They staked out the horses again and gave them a good rub-down, since they didn't bring along a brush.

Kandee slept on her right side to keep an eye on Mystic. Lou slept on her left side to keep an eye on Flash. The ground was a bit damp. The girls had no tent and couldn't carry a ground cloth.

They hummed and sang their horses' songs as they tried to sleep. The sound did seem to lull the horses.

The night was fitful for the girls because of the odd sounds in the woods, the noise of the horses, and their concern that the horses might spook at something unknown.

Perhaps the girls slept a little; perhaps they didn't. They were up at the crack of dawn. The air was quite nippy. The horses seemed to do well in the night and that pleased the girls. Then they looked at each other.

"You look like you broke out in chicken pox during the night," Kandee said to Lou.

"I do? Hey, you do too."

"What do you mean?"

"The left half of your face is covered in red bumps," Lou said to Kandee.

"The right half of your face is covered in red bumps," Kandee said to Lou.

"What is the matter with us?"

The girls began to itch. It turned out the red bumps were mosquito bites. Kandee had slept on her right side towards Mystic, so the bites were on the left side of her face. Lou slept on her left side facing towards Flash, so her bites were on the right side of her face. They thought they looked awful. Oh well, that was the price to pay for all this fun.

The girls decided to eat breakfast, and then ride all day exploring new trails and logging roads as they found them, and maybe they would see if Mystic liked swimming as much as Flash did.

They prepared to eat cold cereal; however, they had forgotten bowls, so they ate by handfuls from the cereal box.

"I hope the horses had enough grass to eat. We should feed them their oats before we leave," they decided.

For most of the morning the girls rode the horses on various logging roads, trails and along the river. They took the horses swimming too. Mystic was hesitant, but followed Flash into the water. The girls tried to perch on the horses' backs because they didn't want to get too wet. They didn't have a towel or change of clothes. Of course, it was impossible to stay dry.

Then they heard what sounded like a motorized vehicle.

"What can that be?" Kandee questioned.

"Oh no, I don't want any other people here to ruin our fun," Lou stated.

They decided they should investigate. As they rounded a bend along the river, they saw Dad's car driving along the bumpy logging road. They rode up to meet him.

"What are you doing here?" Lou asked.

"Why did you come after us?" Kandee wanted to know.

"You told us to be home by supper, and we were planning to do that. Why did you ruin our chance to run away from home, Dad?" Lou asked belligerently.

Dad said, "I know you two are not happy to see me. I'm sorry to spoil your fun, but I thought you'd want to know. Mr. Tony told the owners of the cannery where he takes his berries that you two were good workers, and he put you both in for a job at the cannery. The cannery owner called wondering if you could come in today for an interview. If they hire you, you can start tomorrow. The job will only last a couple of weeks until they process the last of this season's berries."

Lou and Kandee looked at each other in amazement. They were excited at the prospect of a real job! They were disappointed to have their campout ruined. They decided they better try for the job. That way, they could spend a couple more weeks together before school started.

39

The girls loaded their sleeping bags and gear into Dad's car so they could ride home unencumbered.

They sang their songs to the horses as they rode home.

They returned Mystic to Mr. Tony's small field.

"Thanks for a great ride, Mystic," Kandee told him, as she gave him a few berries and patted him dry. Mystic nickered softly as he nudged Kandee's shoulder. He seemed sad to see Kandee leave.

Then the girl's rode double on Flash back home. They put Flash in his pasture after giving him a rub down and a treat. He walked to the center of the pasture with his nose down, rolled on both sides, then stood up and shook vigorously. He began to nibble the grass. The girls watched him a moment and were reluctant to leave. Then in unison, they turned and ran into the house to take a bath and clean up for the interview. Usually they just sat on the side of the tub and washed their feet and legs, but after getting so dirty and grimy from this wonderful camping adventure, they decided they needed the works; a full clean up.

CHAPTER 10

REALITY

The girls were embarrassed about their half mosquito-bitten, red, polka-dotted faces; however, they were offered the job in the cannery.

They worked long hours during the last two weeks of summer. There was no time to ride, and not much time to care for Flash or do other chores.

The first opportunity to go visit Mystic occurred on their first day off. The girls rode double on Flash. They were excited and planned to pick up where they left off exploring the country along the river.

When the girls arrived at Mr. Tony's place, they knew something was wrong. He had a sad face and did not appear to be glad to see them. There was no whinnying welcome either.

"What's the matter? Where's Mystic?" Kandee asked.

"I'm sorry to tell you girls this," said Mr. Tony, "but the owners came and took him away. They said they found a place to keep him near where they live at the beach."

Kandee was inconsolable. "I didn't even get to say good-bye," she cried. "He is the best horse in the world. I had the best time of my life with him. I wanted to buy him. Now I don't even know where he is."

"Please, Mr. Tony, help us find him," Lou begged with grief.

"I'll see what I can do," he offered doubtfully. "You are good girls, and I know you really care for him. I told the owners how you helped me take care of him this summer. I know they were appreciative."

That was little consolation to the two sad girls. They swung up on Flash, once again their one and only trusted steed. Flash seemed sad too, as he lowered his head and slowly trod home.

EPILOGUE

TIME FLEW

That summer ended.

Kandee stayed in the city and attended high school there. Lou lived in the country and attended the local high school. The girls never attended school together, but thanks in part to Brian who helped with transportation, the girls remained best friends over the years.

After a couple of years making trips to the beach in efforts to find Mystic, Kandee did eventually get a horse of her own. Honeycomb was a beautiful bay mare who looked like a matching bookend to Flash. Lou and Kandee enjoyed the similarity of their horses. They bought white bridles and sometimes dressed alike when they went riding. Lou and Flash, Kandee and Honeycomb had many other amazing riding adventures.

The girls grew up, went their separate ways, married, raised families, moved to various locations in other states, held jobs, and accepted many responsibilities over the years. Throughout their lives each even had a series of other horses to love.

After Lou grew up and moved away, Flash had other owners. Each owner provided him a good home. Lou met each of the owners in turn. She made sure they knew how special he was and showed them how he would do his tricks. Whenever possible, Lou, sometimes with Kandee, visited Flash throughout his long and happy life.

Lou and Kandee remained friends over the years, and still visit on occasion.

On one long-ago visit, Dad was also visiting. He bounced Kandee's young son on his knee, while her other son played with Lou's two boys on the floor at his feet. Dad remarked, "You two girls grew up to be pretty good mothers. I guess I should've known you would since you took such good care of Flash, that old nag of yours."

Somehow, even all these years later, hearing Flash called a "nag" raised the ire in the women.

"Now Dad," Lou interjected as she lovingly patted his arm, "You know Flash was more magnificent than your powerful, golden palomino stallion and was truly one of the greatest horses ever born."

"Yes, he was," Kandee added definitively, and Dad reluctantly agreed.

The young children looked at their mothers and Granddad with a blank stare, then returned their attention to their toys.

Many years later during a recent visit, Kandee and Lou, now grandmothers, sipped their tea. Kandee and her husband, Spence, had recently celebrated their Silver Anniversary. Lou and Brian were about to celebrate their own Silver Anniversary. The women discussed their families and the events currently happening in their lives. It wasn't long before they drifted into conversation about their chance meeting on a school bus and how incredible it was that they ever met and became lifelong friends. They reminisced about their time with those magnificent horses, Flashing Arrow and Mystic Phantom, the horses that had become their real "dream herd."

"You know, I feel that first summer with those horses was the pivotal point of my growing up years. So much happened that was special," Lou stated.

Kandee agreed. "That summer was so fantastic. It was one of the best times of my life. It made me realize dreams do come true, and even though one dream may not last, if I keep dreaming, other dreams will come true, too."

Lou agreed. "I've kept the idea, 'Keep Dreaming' as my motto through the years, too."

As she adjusted her glasses, Kandee sighed, "I've sure enjoyed this visit. I love our youthful adventures, and it is fun to remember them. The older we get, the better those times seem."

Lou took a sip of tea. She nodded her white head in agreement. "Times have really changed. Nowadays, young people don't have the opportunity to pick berries or hold other jobs because of the change in labor laws. Berry-picking machines are even used. Also, I don't think I would let my kids take off and go camping alone in remote wild areas, even with the availability of cell phones. People are not so trustworthy these days and the world does not seem so kind."

Kandee agreed. "Kids these days don't know what they are missing. I feel sorry for them, but I suppose they enjoy other interests and entertainment. Today's kids have so much technology available to them."

Lou added, "They also have 4-H and high school equestrian teams, which are great programs, although very structured. Today's kids are lucky to have horse-related programs. I would've like that."

The women decided the times of their own life were most unique, not as strict as it was for their parents and not as regulated as it is for their children. "I wonder how it will be for the grandkids," they pondered.

They decided to toast their good fortune to have grown up in good times.

"Here's to a wonderful childhood with wonderful horses," Lou toasted with her tea cup.

"Here's to enjoying life then and now," Kandee added her toast, and then drank her last drop of tea.

"I have something to show you," Lou told Kandee. She walked into her bedroom and retrieved a long wooden box from behind her dresser. She opened the box to show Kandee the horse tail that she had cut off Flash when he injured himself those long years ago. She held up the black tail, still shiny and smooth after all these years.

"Brian made this wooden box for me when we married, and I have kept Flash's tail in it ever since," Lou told Kandee. "This is my most precious keepsake."

Kandee fingered the tail reverently. "I remember the feel of him, she whispered softly."

"Me too," Lou breathed. "It still smells like Flash." With a tear in her eye, she reluctantly laid the tail in the box and placed it back behind the dresser.

Then Kandee said, "Do you remember the old plow bit we found in the field that we used for Mystic? I have it hanging on my bedroom wall. It's my special keepsake."

The women sighed at the memories.

"Thinking about all the fun we had riding those magnificent horses makes me want to get out and go for a ride now. Are you up for that?" Lou asked Kandee, as they walked back into the kitchen.

Kandee agreed eagerly. "Let's go saddle up. Meet you in the barn."

As they put on their helmets and boots and saddled the magnificent steeds that they rode today, they discussed where they wanted to ride.

"Let's explore that new equestrian park recently developed," Lou suggested.

Kandee said, "I guess we haven't changed too much over the years. Now we just use a saddle, a helmet and ride a little slower. No more bareback races in cut-off jeans and bare feet."

Lou said, "Those rides were exhilarating! There will never be another summer as wonderful as our first summer with horses."

"But thank God we can still ride," they said in unison, as they trotted along.

This story is based on true events.

CPSIA information can be obtained
at www.ICGtesting.com
Printed in the USA
FFHW022046181119
56085719-62111FF